HE'S YOUNG,
HE'S HANDSOME,
HE'S *TOTALLY* COOL.

He's Mr. Smock, the new art teacher at Bear Country School, and Queenie has a crush on him, big time! To prove it, she paints a great big heart with a Cupid's arrow through it and "Q & S" written across it.

Funny, Queenie's boyfriend's name doesn't begin with S. It begins with T. That's double T, for Too-Tall Grizzly. When Too-Tall finds out who "S" is, there's going to be trouble in Bear Country, the kind that only Too-Tall can stir up!

BIG CHAPTER BOOKS

The Berenstain Bears and the Drug Free Zone
The Berenstain Bears and the New Girl in Town
The Berenstain Bears Gotta Dance!
The Berenstain Bears and the Nerdy Nephew
The Berenstain Bears Accept No Substitutes
The Berenstain Bears and the Female Fullback
The Berenstain Bears and the Red-Handed Thief
The Berenstain Bears
    and the Wheelchair Commando
The Berenstain Bears and the School Scandal Sheet
The Berenstain Bears and the Galloping Ghost
The Berenstain Bears at Camp Crush
The Berenstain Bears and the Giddy Grandma
The Berenstain Bears and the Dress Code
The Berenstain Bears' Media Madness
The Berenstain Bears in the Freaky Funhouse
The Berenstain Bears
    and the Showdown at Chainsaw Gap
The Berenstain Bears at the Teen Rock Cafe
The Berenstain Bears in Maniac Mansion
The Berenstain Bears and the Bermuda Triangle
The Berenstain Bears
    and the Ghost of the Auto Graveyard
The Berenstain Bears and the Haunted Hayride

The Berenstain Bears
and
QUEENIE'S
CRAZY
CRUSH

by the Berenstains

A BIG CHAPTER BOOK™

Random House New York

Copyright © 1997 by Berenstain Enterprises, Inc.
All rights reserved under International and Pan-American Copyright Conventions. Published in the United States by Random House, Inc., New York, and simultaneously in Canada by Random House of Canada Limited, Toronto.

http://www.randomhouse.com/

Library of Congress Cataloging-in-Publication Data
Berenstain, Stan, 1923–
The Berenstain Bears and Queenie's crazy crush / by the Berenstains.
    p. cm. — (A big chapter book)
Summary: When Queenie McBear gets a crush on her new art teacher, her boyfriend gets jealous, and learns how to paint in the process.
ISBN 0-679-88745-8 (trade). — ISBN 0-679-98745-2 (lib. bdg.)
[1. Bears—Fiction. 2. Schools—Fiction. 3. Teacher-student relationships—Fiction. 4. Painting—Fiction.] I. Berenstain, Jan, 1923– .
II. Title. III. Series: Berenstain, Stan, 1923– . Big chapter book.
PZ7.B4483Beaj 1997
[Fic]—dc21
97-15587

Printed in the United States of America 10 9 8 7 6 5 4 3 2 1

BIG CHAPTER BOOKS is a trademark of Berenstain Enterprises, Inc.

Contents

Chapter 1
Mr. Smock

Year after year, cubs' most common complaint about Bear Country School was that nothing ever changed. "How was school today?" a parent would ask. And the cub would shrug and say, "Same as usual." For the most part, it was true. Same school building, same playground, same classrooms, same blackboards. Same teachers, same staff, same coaches, same principal.

Even the same complaints. Yes, that's right. Believe it or not, Bear Country School's cubs even complained that their own complaints never changed.

But change something—change just one little thing at school—and what happened? More complaints! "Why did they move the bulletin board down the hall?" a cub would say. "Yeah," another would add. "What was wrong with it where it was?" That's because, down deep, most cubs really didn't *want* anything to change. Whether they realized it or not, they found it sort of comforting that the bulletin boards and the bike racks were always in the same place. (Almost

always, that is.) And it was also comforting to think that Mr. Honeycomb would always be sitting behind his big wooden desk in the principal's office and that Mr. Grizzmeyer's bullhorn voice would always be heard yelling at players out on the football field.

It was especially comforting that the teachers rarely changed. It was hard to imagine Bear Country School without Teacher Bob or Teacher Jane, or even without Miss Glitch. As much as the cubs complained about having the same old teachers year in and year out, nothing upset them more than a teacher retiring or moving away. And that's exactly what happened when Mrs. Palette retired.

Mrs. Palette had been the art teacher at Bear Country School for as long as anyone could remember. And that's no exaggeration. For it wasn't only the current generation of cubs that had been taught art by Mrs. Palette. Earlier generations had, too. Papa and Mama Bear had been taught art at Bear Country School by Mrs. Palette, and

so had Two-Ton and Too-Too Grizzly. Farmer and Mrs. Ben had been taught by Mrs. Palette, and they were pretty old. Even Dr. Gert Grizzly had, and she was even older. It seemed that everyone in Beartown, at one time or another, had done an art project under the watchful eye of Mrs. Palette or viewed her slide lecture on "Great Works of Art in the History of Bear-kind."

So it came as quite a shock when, at the close of a school year, Mrs. Palette announced her retirement. Over the summer months that followed, cubs occasionally wondered out loud who the new art teacher would be. What would she be like? Would she be young or old? Tall or short? Strict or easygoing?

When at last the cubs filed into the school auditorium for the first assembly of

the new school year, most of their questions were answered. Seated beside Mr. Honeycomb on the stage was a bear wearing a purple beret and a brown smock-jacket over a purple turtleneck. It was obvious that this was the new art teacher, for the smock-jacket was covered with paint smears. That was something different. Mrs. Palette's clothes had always been spotless. But there was something else different about the new art teacher that everyone noticed right away. Especially the girl cubs. "It's a he!"

Babs Bruno whispered to Queenie McBear. "The new art teacher is a *he!*"

Queenie was staring at the stage as though she were in the middle of a beautiful daydream. At first, Babs thought she hadn't heard. But after a moment, Queenie murmured, "Yes, and a *young* he...a young and *handsome* he...."

Mr. Honeycomb rose and strode to the lectern. "Good morning, cubs," he said into the microphone. "This morning I would like to introduce someone to you. We are honored and privileged to have Mr. Smock as our new art teacher at Bear Country School. 'Privileged' because Mr. Smock is a fine teacher of cubs. 'Honored' because he is an up-and-coming artist whose name will soon be known throughout Bear Country."

"Wow!" said Babs, who liked art almost as much as she liked poetry.

"Cool!" said Queenie, who liked art a lot more than poetry.

"Mr. Smock has had many of his paintings on display in galleries in Big Bear City," Mr. Honeycomb continued. "He is currently hard at work on a large oil painting for the Bear Country Museum of Fine Art. And he has graciously promised our students and faculty the very first look at this master-piece. I would like Mr. Smock to make the exciting announcement personally."

Mr. Smock replaced the principal at the

lectern. "My new painting is nearly finished," he said. "I will unveil it at the end of a special fine arts assembly next week."

There were "oohs" and "aahs" from a number of cubs in the audience, including Babs and Queenie. But not everyone was so impressed. Ferdy Factual folded his arms across his tweed jacket and said, "Good heavens. The Ego has landed."

Queenie, who was sitting in the row in front of Ferdy, turned on him. *"Ego!"* she hissed. "Of all the cubs who shouldn't talk

about big egos, you're first on the list! Besides, I'll bet Mr. Honeycomb talked him into it."

"I can't imagine why you're so impressed with this fellow," said Ferdy. "If he's such a big shot in the art world, then what is he doing here teaching a bunch of cubs how to make collages?"

"You heard Mr. Honeycomb," snapped Queenie. "*Up-and-coming* big shot."

Now Too-Tall Grizzly, sitting two rows behind Queenie, spoke up. "Oh, he's a big shot, all right. He just *shot* off his *big* mouth about his great unveiling!"

"Hey, boss," said Skuzz. "He don't need to unveil his masterpiece."

"Why not?" asked Too-Tall.

"'Cause he's *wearin'* it!" said Skuzz. "Ha ha ha!"

Smirk and Vinnie joined in laughing, but

Too-Tall stopped them. "Cool it, guys," he said. "Teacher Bob's givin' us the evil eye."

But Teacher Bob wasn't the only one giving them the evil eye. So was Queenie. "You bums couldn't tell a masterpiece from a road sign," she sneered.

"Aw, come on, Queenie," chided Too-Tall. "Ya gotta admit he looks pretty ridiculous in those silly clothes."

Queenie tilted her head back and looked down her nose at Too-Tall. "*I* think he looks kind of cute!" she said, and turned back to the stage.

At first, Too-Tall felt a pang of jealousy that made him sit straight up and glare at the bear at the lectern. After all, Queenie was his on-again, off-again girlfriend. Naturally, it bothered him whenever she called another guy "cute." But then he settled back in his seat and relaxed. *She got me again*, he thought. *She just says those things to make me jealous.* Besides, Mr. Smock was just a teacher, not another cub....

Chapter 2
Q & S

"All right, cubs, settle down," said Mr. Smock. "Let's get started."

Teacher Bob's class was having its first art period of the year. Every year, Mrs. Palette had started with her slide lecture on "Great Works of Art in the History of Bearkind." But this year would be different. No slide projector or screen had been set up. Instead, the art room was ringed with a dozen easels.

"We'll be working with a number of different materials over the course of the year," said Mr. Smock. "But since I'm a

painter first and foremost, we'll begin with painting. By the end of the year, each of you will complete an oil painting. You'll be glad to know that I will supply you with oil paints, brushes, canvases, and everything else you'll need. But today we'll paint with watercolors. I want you to take turns at the easels painting anything that interests you. Then we'll have a look at each painting."

The cubs busied themselves with paint-

ing. Near the end of the period, each cub in turn held up his or her painting for the whole class to see. Some were good, others not so good. But Mr. Smock found something encouraging to say about each one. Almost each one, that is.

When Brother Bear held up a painting of a football player, Mr. Smock said, "Good strong brush strokes. Obviously, Brother is interested in sports."

Babs held up her portrait of William Shakesbear. "Fine," said Mr. Smock. "You've got the shape of the head just right, Babs. Would I be correct in guessing that you're interested in poetry?" Babs nodded.

Ferdy's painting showed a bear holding a test tube in a science laboratory. "Excellent attention to detail, Ferdy," said Mr. Smock. "From the tweed jacket and knickers your figure is wearing, I'd guess that this is a painting of you as a scientist."

"Wrong," said Ferdy icily. "It's my uncle, Actual Factual, the great scientist, in his laboratory at the Bearsonian Institution. Of which he is the director, I might add. Of course, the painting might well have been

of me, since I often do high-level work in my uncle's lab."

"I see," said Mr. Smock. "From your painting, I'd say that you're interested in science, Ferdy. And from your explanation of it, I'd say you are also very interested in *yourself*."

The other cubs all laughed. Ferdy, with a shrug and a yawn, put on his best bored expression.

Skuzz had done a painting of a frowning face with a black eye. "Hmm," said Mr. Smock. "Skuzz must think of himself as kind of a tough guy."

Too-Tall's painting was exactly like Skuzz's, except that the face had two black

eyes instead of one. "Too-Tall must be a friend of Skuzz's," said Mr. Smock. "And his interests appear to run along the same lines."

Smirk and Vinnie held up identical paintings. Actually, they weren't paintings at all. They were blank sheets of white paper. "Well, well," joked Mr. Smock. "Here we have a couple of landscape paintings—of the North Pole."

Smirk made an obnoxious noise like the "wrong" buzzer on a TV quiz show. "Sorry, Teach," he said. "Only Vinnie's is of the North Pole. Mine is of the *South* Pole."

"Yeah," said Vinnie. "We didn't want to paint the same picture."

"I see," said Mr. Smock. "Obviously, you two are interested in making fun of new teachers." He looked straight at Smirk. "And from the goofy expression on your

face, I can see why they call you Smirk."

That got another laugh from the rest of the class. Smirk even blushed for a second.

Queenie's painting was last. Wearing a dreamy smile, she held up a picture of a big bulging heart with a Cupid's arrow through it. In the center of the heart she had printed Q & S.

"Hmm," said Mr. Smock. "Can you all see how Queenie has made the heart three-dimensional by painting it darker here and lighter there? Very well done, Queenie." Queenie beamed. "And I think it's pretty clear what Queenie is interested in: a cub whose name starts with S."

Bonnie Brown leaned over to Brother and whispered, "What's *interesting* about that is that her boyfriend's name begins with T!"

Brother looked over at Too-Tall. He was staring at Queenie's painting with teeth and fists clenched. "Uh-oh," whispered Brother. "When Too-Tall finds out who S is, that cub's gonna be in big trouble."

"And *until* he finds out," said Bonnie, "every boy cub whose first name starts with S is gonna be in big trouble!"

Chapter 3
A Snake in the Grass

No sooner had the Too-Tall gang exited the art room than Too-Tall backed Skuzz up against the hallway wall. "All right, Skuzzo," he snarled. "Got anything you wanna tell me?"

Skuzz looked quickly at Smirk and Vinnie, then back at Too-Tall. "Whaddya mean, boss? Tell ya what?"

"Well, now," said Too-Tall. "Let's you and me pretend we're Nerdy Ferdy and his uncle and figure it out with logic."

Skuzz's knees started to shake. "Uh, er...okay, boss," he stammered. "Which one am I? Ferdy or his uncle?"

"It don't matter, dummy!" growled Too-Tall. "All that matters is the logic!" He put his hands on his hips and pushed his nose right into Skuzz's face. "Now, let's see. Queenie just wrote Q & S on a big heart with a Cupid's arrow through it. That must mean she's got a crush on somebody whose name starts with S. Right?"

AND SO DOES "SNAKE IN THE GRASS"

"Uh...er...yeah, boss, I follow ya," said Skuzz.

"Good. Now, Queenie's my girlfriend. But her new crush ain't on me. How do we know that?"

Skuzz thought hard. He was sweating as well as shaking now. "Er...I know, boss...'cause your name don't start with S!"

"Right! You ain't as dumb as I thought, birdbrain! Now, listen up. Since she's my girlfriend, Queenie hangs around us gang members a lot. And you are one of those gang members. And your name, 'Skuzz,' starts with an S. And so does 'snake in the grass,' which means a guy who tries to steal somebody's girlfriend!" Too-Tall's left hand still rested on his hip, but now he had bunched his right hand into a huge fist and was holding it right in Skuzz's face.

"No, boss!" cried Skuzz. "It wasn't me! I

swear! I don't even *like* Queenie!"

"You *what*?" roared Too-Tall.

"No, wait, that came out backward, boss! I meant, *she* don't even like *me!* Yeah, that's it, boss...that's what I meant! She's always liked Smirk better than me...hey, wait ...*Smirk starts with an S, too!*"

"That's right, boss!" said Vinnie. But Smirk had nothing to say. Because Smirk was nowhere to be seen.

Too-Tall lowered his fist and looked around. "Where is that little snake in the grass?" he said.

"I'll bet that's exactly where he is," said Vinnie.

"Where?"

"Out hiding in the tall grass at the edge of the football field," said Vinnie.

"Let's go," said Too-Tall.

"What about Teacher Bob's class, boss?" asked Skuzz.

"Gang business before school business" was Too-Tall's decision.

Moments later the three gang members were at the edge of the football field, standing before a patch of tall grass and weeds. Raising his voice enough for anyone hiding in the grass to hear, Too-Tall said, "Watch out when you walk through this tall grass, guys! *Sometimes snakes hide in it!*" And with that, Too-Tall walked into the tall grass and motioned for the others to join him.

The three of them stomped around in the tall grass. Pretty soon there was an "Ouch!"

"Well, well, what have we here?" said Too-Tall, grasping Smirk by the collar and pulling him from underfoot. "It's a snake! A big brown *furry* snake!" With one huge hand he held Smirk at arm's length. "What're ya doin' down there in the grass, Smirk? Collectin' ants for an ant farm? Huntin' grasshoppers for your lunch?"

Smirk shook even harder than Skuzz had earlier in the hallway. "I...I g-got scared, bboss...when I realized my n-name starts with S...."

Vinnie decided it was time to rescue Smirk. Bravely he stepped up to Too-Tall and whispered in his ear: "He didn't do it, boss. Think about it. How could Queenie ever prefer that little whimpering fool to you?"

"Hmm," said Too-Tall. "You've got a point there."

"Sure, boss," said Vinnie. "Skuzz only pointed a finger at Smirk to get you off his own back. Look at him. He's still shakin'!"

Too-Tall looked from one shivering gang member to the other. He lowered Smirk to the ground and let go. "Sorry I lost my temper, guys," he said. "I shoulda known neither of you bums would have the guts to steal my girlfriend. But we still have to find out who did!"

"You bet, boss!" said Vinnie. "How about if you take the sixth grade, Skuzz takes the fifth, Smirk the fourth, and I take the second?"

"What happened to the third grade?" said Too-Tall.

" 'Second' begins with an S!" said Vinnie.

"So does 'stupid'!" bellowed Too-Tall. "So maybe I should question *you!* Look, there's no way Queenie's gonna get a crush on a second grader. I think we should concentrate on fifth and sixth graders. She goes for the older cubs."

"Yeah, like you, boss!" said Skuzz.

Vinnie gave Skuzz a puzzled look. "But *his* name don't start with an S..."

Chapter 4
Too-Tall's Spy

Too-Tall and the gang put their plan into action immediately. In the school halls, at recess, and on the way home, they cornered every older boy cub whose name started with S. There was a lot of shaking and quaking before they were through. But not one of the cubs would admit to being Queenie's new crush. So the next morning, before

Queenie arrived at the schoolyard, the gang questioned all of her girlfriends from Teacher Bob's class. Maybe she had told one of them who S was. But...no luck.

"I think we're going about this the wrong way, boss," said Skuzz.

"What d'ya mean?" said Too-Tall.

"Queenie must have a *secret* crush, boss. That means Queenie is the only one who knows who it is."

"So what do you suggest I do?" asked Too-Tall.

It would have been logical to suggest that Too-Tall go up to Queenie and ask her who S was. But when it came to Too-Tall's feelings about Queenie, logic wasn't much help. Skuzz, Smirk, and Vinnie all knew there were only two bears in all Bear Country that Too-Tall was afraid of. One was his dad, Two-Ton. The other was Queenie. He was always afraid that Queenie would get mad at him for something. And prying into her secret crush might just be one of those things. So the gang was taking no chances. They tried hard to think of some other way of finding out who S was.

As he thought, Skuzz happened to look across the schoolyard. Suddenly his eyes lit up. "Hey, boss!" he said. "There's Bermuda McBear hangin' out with Cool Carl King!"

"Too bad," joked Too-Tall. "She oughta stay away from that dude."

"That's not what I meant, boss," said Skuzz. "Bermuda is Queenie's cousin. She even lives with Queenie. Maybe you could get her to find out who S is."

Too-Tall smiled. "Good thinkin', skuzz-brain," he said. He sidled over to Bermuda. "Hey, there, Bermuda McBear. How're things goin'?"

"Not bad, big guy," said Bermuda. "I'd ask you the same thing, but I'm afraid to."

Too-Tall nodded. "Yeah," he said. "I'm pretty upset about this Q & S business. You know what I'm talkin' about?"

"Who doesn't?" said Bermuda.

"Has Queenie said anything to you about it?"

Bermuda shook her head. "Sorry, big guy."

"Look," said Too-Tall. "I'll bet you can find out who S is. It's probably some older

I'LL OWE YOU A FAVOR.
BIG TIME.

cub. Talk to Queenie tonight. Draw it out of her. Then report to me here in the morning. I'll owe you a favor. Big time."

Bermuda shrugged. "I don't know," she said. "If I find out who this S cub is, what're you gonna do to him?"

"Just threaten him a little," said Too-Tall. "I ain't gonna hurt him. Won't have to. Everybody's scared of me." He looked at Cool Carl. "Right, Cool?"

Cool smiled and said, "Right, big guy." Cool Carl was cool, but his notion of "cool" didn't include messing with Too-Tall.

"Okay," said Bermuda. "It's a deal."

Chapter 5
New News Is Bad News

The next morning, Bermuda reached the schoolyard before anyone else. She came early because she was worried. She needed to talk to someone. Anyone.

Ferdy and his girlfriend, Trudy Brunowitz, were next to arrive.

"Trudy!" cried Bermuda. "Am I glad to see *you!* I need to talk to you before Too-Tall gets here."

"What's up?" asked Trudy.

"Look, you're the smartest girl in the school," said Bermuda. "You can tell me what to do. I promised Too-Tall I'd find out from Queenie who S is. Well, I did. I'm supposed to tell him as soon as he gets here. But I'm afraid of what he might do."

"Why?" asked Trudy. "Who is it?" Bermuda hesitated. "If I'm going to help you," Trudy prodded, "you have to tell me."

Bermuda let out a big sigh. "S stands for Smock," she said.

Trudy stared. "Smock? As in Mr. Smock? Our art teacher?"

"Bingo," said Bermuda.

"Oh, dear," said Trudy. "I see your problem."

"What problem?" asked Ferdy.

"She's afraid that Too-Tall will do something to Mr. Smock and get kicked out of school," said Trudy.

"Nonsense," said Ferdy. "Too-Tall will do nothing of the kind. As soon as he hears that Queenie's crush is a hopeless one that can lead nowhere, he'll realize that Mr. Smock is no threat to his own position as Queenie's boyfriend. It is only logical that Too-Tall will then forget all about Queenie's crazy crush."

"I don't know about that, Ferd," said Trudy. "Love and jealousy aren't rocket science, you know. That kind of logic doesn't always work."

"Don't be silly," said Ferdy. "Too-Tall may be a jerk, but he's not stupid. Look, here he comes now. Too-Tall! Hey, Too-Tall!"

Too-Tall and the gang came over. Ferdy gave Bermuda a nudge and said, "Bermuda has something important to tell you, big guy."

"I've been waitin' all night for this," said

Too-Tall, with a wicked grin. "Well, let's have it."

Bermuda's face broke into a big sheepish smile. "Er...uh...I really like your cap, Too-Tall."

"That's not it!" said Ferdy. He poked Bermuda in the ribs. "Go on. Tell him who S is."

"Well...okay," said Bermuda. "Remember how you thought it was an older cub, big guy? Well, you were *half* right. He is older. But he's not a cub."

Too-Tall glared at Bermuda. "Oh, he ain't a cub? So what is he, a frog?"

The gang snickered at that, but they stopped the moment Bermuda said, "Smock."

Too-Tall's glare turned into a blank stare. For a moment he said nothing. Finally he got his mouth open. "*Smock?*" he said. "As in Mr. Smock? Our *art teacher?* The silly guy with the purple beret and the paint-smeared jacket?"

"Isn't that great?" said Ferdy. "It's just a crazy crush. Smock could never feel the same way about Queenie. And as soon as she realizes that, she'll forget all about him. Isn't that a relief?"

But Too-Tall didn't look relieved. He looked upset. And confused. *Really* confused. "I don't get it," he said. "Queenie already has me, a real stud. What does she want with that wimpy artist?"

"It all depends on whose eyes you're seeing things through," said Bermuda. "You look at yourself and you see a stud. You look at Mr. Smock and you see a wimp. But Queenie loves art. Naturally, she's attracted to artistic types. And who could be more artistic than a painter who's painting a masterpiece for the Bear Country Museum of Fine Art? So, when Queenie looks at Mr. Smock, she sees a stud. And when she looks at you, she sees a wimp. An *art* wimp. Hey, don't look so glum, big guy. What's wrong? Didn't I explain it well enough?"

"Cool it!" Trudy hissed at Bermuda. "You explained it *too* well!"

"Oh, sorry, big guy," said Bermuda. "I didn't mean to hurt your feelings."

But it was too late for apologies. Too-Tall, shoulders hunched and head down, was already trudging off toward the schoolyard gate.

Chapter 6
Too-Tall's Great Idea

Too-Tall wasn't seen again at school all that day. No one knew where he'd gone. He hadn't even told the other gang members. So after school, Skuzz decided they should split up to search. His plan was simple. He would check the gang's clubhouse behind Parts R Us, Two-Ton's auto-parts lot. Smirk would check Biff Bruin's Pharmacy and the Burger Bear. And Vinnie, who was so dim-witted that he might forget where he was going on the way there, would search wher-ever he wanted. At five o'clock they would meet at the Burger Bear.

A few minutes before five, Skuzz walked into the Burger Bear to see Smirk sitting alone in the gang's favorite booth. It turned out that neither of them had found Too-Tall. They waited a whole hour for Vinnie, but he never showed up. So they went home.

The next morning, Vinnie was the last of the three to get to the corner of Main and Elm, where the gang always met to walk to school together.

"Well, well," said Skuzz, "if it ain't Little Boy Lost. Don't tell me: you stopped to take a quick nap in some vacant lot and didn't wake up until this morning."

"Sorry I couldn't make it yesterday," said Vinnie. "I was runnin' errands for the boss."

"You found him!" said Smirk.

"So where was he?" asked Skuzz.

"Sittin' on a rock out in the woods behind

school," said Vinnie. "There's a little rocky
clearing that Brother Bear calls his Thinking Place. The boss said he decided to try it
out 'cause he needed to think. And it must
have worked."

"What did he come up with?" asked Smirk.

"Wouldn't tell me," said Vinnie. "But I know he got an idea, 'cause right after I got there he jumped up and said something very strange."

"What was it?" asked Skuzz.

"I memorized it word for word," said Vinnie. "Hang on..." He closed his eyes and gritted his teeth. "Oh, yeah! He said, 'If it's art that Queenie wants, then art she shall have!' Just like that. Weirdest thing that ever came out of his mouth."

"And then what did he do?" asked Skuzz.

"He told me to go get some things for him," said Vinnie. "First I hit the art closet at school: all kinds of oil paints, brushes, canvases, a palette, even an easel. Then my mom's china closet: a cut-glass vase and a china bowl. Next, I hit our garage for a lantern. Last, the supermarket: one bag of oranges. Then I took everything to the boss over at the clubhouse."

"Did you ask him what he was gonna do with all that stuff?" asked Smirk.

"Yeah," said Vinnie.

"What did he say?"

"He said, 'Shut up and get outta here before I break yer face.' "

"Well," said Smirk, "at least he's still his old bossy self. What do you think he's up to?"

"Probably gonna sell all that stuff so he can buy Queenie a nice present," said Vinnie.

Skuzz threw his head back and laughed. "*Sell* it?" he cried. "You two dummies are lucky I'm around to tell you the difference between your heads and your elbows. It's *obvious* what the boss is doin'. He's paintin' a picture!"

"Of what?" said Vinnie.

"Of a cut-glass vase and a bowl of

oranges, you nitwit!" said Skuzz. "And since he had you steal him a lantern, I'll bet he's been paintin' all night."

Vinnie still looked puzzled. "Why's he paintin' a picture? He don't even like art."

"What Bermuda said about him bein' an art wimp must have gotten to him," said Skuzz. "So he's tryin' to win Queenie's heart back by outpainting Mr. Smock."

"He's nuts!" said Smirk. "There's no way he can outpaint Smock!"

"You know what they say," said Skuzz. *"Love is blind."*

Chapter 7
The First Unveiling

That morning, just before lunch, Teacher Bob's class had their second art period of the new school year. This time they made collages. Near the end of class, Mr. Smock called for everyone's attention and pointed to Queenie. "Since you were last to show your watercolor painting," he said, "it's only fair that you be the first to show your collage."

"Thank you, Mr. Smock," said Queenie. She skipped to the front of the room and held up her collage. It was the same as her watercolor painting. But this time the heart was of colored paper, the arrow had been cut out of a magazine photo, and the letters Q & S were made of tiny glued-on shells.

"Very nice," said Mr. Smock. "You know, class, there's nothing wrong with doing the same picture twice. Many great artists have treated the same subject over and over with different materials, from different angles, in different lighting. All right. Babs may go next."

But Queenie didn't seem to want to sit down. She gazed dreamily up at Mr. Smock and said, "It's a picture of a heart. And it's also *from* the heart..."

There were titters and giggles from the class. By now, Mr. Smock was the only bear in the room who didn't know who S was.

Mr. Smock smiled. "That's very sweet, Queenie," he said.

Queenie sighed and said, "Not *half* as sweet as S."

The tittering and giggling got louder. What was she doing? Was she going to tell Mr. Smock she had a crush on him? Right there in front of the whole class?

Just then the door swung open and in marched Too-Tall, carrying a large canvas. He snatched up an easel, took it to the front

of the room, and placed the canvas on it. Over the canvas was draped one of Too-Too's aprons. He looked tired, as if he hadn't slept a wink. But he also had a proud grin on his face.

"If there's gonna be any unveiling of masterpieces around here," he announced, "it's gonna be right here, right now!" And, with that, he whipped the apron from the canvas, like a magician performing an amazing trick.

When Too-Tall first burst into the room, Mr. Smock thought of sending him straight to Mr. Grizzmeyer's office for being late and disrupting the class. But now, as he looked at Too-Tall's painting, he began to have second thoughts. Yes, Too-Tall had disrupted the class. But what an odd way to do it! The cub had obviously put a lot of time and effort into his painting. It appeared to be the first oil painting he'd ever done, and it also looked as if he'd done it all by himself, without anyone to show him the tricks of the trade. The painting would surely never hang on the walls of the Bear Country Museum of Fine Art. But for a first try it

was pretty good. Good enough for Mr. Smock to recognize a cut-glass vase and a bowl of some sort of purplish fruit. He decided to go easy on Too-Tall, at least until he could figure out what was going on with the cub.

"Well, class," said Mr. Smock. "We were going to leave oil painting until the end of the year, but it looks as if Too-Tall just couldn't wait." He walked over to the painting. "He's done a kind of painting called a still life. Here we have a cut-glass vase— very difficult to paint, I might add—and here is a bowl of fruit. I can't quite make out the kind of fruit, though. Are they plums, Too-Tall?"

Too-Tall blushed. "No," he said. "They're supposed to be oranges."

The whole class laughed, even the rest of the gang. Too-Tall glared out at everyone,

THEY'RE SUPPOSED TO BE ORANGES.

finally fixing his gaze on Vinnie. "And they woulda *looked* like oranges, too," he said, "if the lamebrain who stole—er, *bought*—the paints for me hadn't forgotten to get orange!"

More laughter.

"But you can make orange," said Mr. Smock. "By mixing what two colors, class?"

Queenie's hand shot up first. "Red and yellow!" she said.

Too-Tall's blush got deeper. "Oh," he mumbled. "I thought it was...red and blue."

"Wrong!" snarled Queenie. "That makes *purple!*" She pointed gleefully at Too-Tall's purple oranges as the class broke into laughter again.

Mr. Smock waved his arms for quiet. He wanted to point out some of the good features of Too-Tall's painting. But before he had the chance, Too-Tall grabbed it and stomped out of the room.

Chapter 8
The Opposite Approach

This time Too-Tall wasn't gone for just a day. He was gone for several days. The gang knew exactly where he was, though. He was holed up in the clubhouse. But he wouldn't let them in. For three days they went to the clubhouse and knocked on the door, and for three days Too-Tall growled at them to leave him alone. By the time they knocked again on the fourth day, they were really starting to worry about their poor boss.

"It's open," they heard Too-Tall say.

They found him pacing the floor. "No

more Mr. Nice Guy," he was grumbling. "No more friendly competition. It's time to pull out all the stops!" He turned and faced the gang. "I tried to win Queenie back by making myself look good, and it didn't work. Now I'm gonna use the opposite approach."

Vinnie frowned. "Make yourself look *bad*, boss?"

"No, goofball!" cried Too-Tall. "Make *Mr. Smock* look bad!"

"Yeah, boss," said Skuzz. "I been thinkin' about that. Remember what we did to Ms. Barr, that substitute teacher, last year? We could rig up another bucket of water in the art room ceiling—"

"Nah!" said Too-Tall. "If we pull the same stunt, everybody'll know who did it. It's gotta be different. And I've got a doozie in mind. One that won't just make Smock look bad, but'll make Queenie hate him for the rest of her life!" He handed Skuzz a sheet of notebook paper and a tape measure. "Here are the measurements of Smock's so-called masterpiece. I sneaked into the auditorium last night to check it out; it's already on the stage for tomorrow's big unveiling. I want you to take this tape measure, sneak into the art closet at school, and get me a canvas exactly the same size."

"What're you gonna do, boss?" asked Smirk.

"Never mind," said Too-Tall. "For now all I'll say is, if you think my days as a painter are over, you've got another think comin'!"

Chapter 9
The Second Unveiling

Mr. Smock sat calmly on a folding chair on the auditorium stage, waiting for Mr. Honeycomb to finish his long-winded speech. Beside him stood the easel that held his veiled masterpiece. The fine-arts assembly was almost over. In a few moments, he would unveil his masterpiece for all to see.

Not just for the students and faculty, though. The press was there, too. Newspaper reporters lined the auditorium walls; photographers and camerabears were crowded into the narrow space in front of the stage.

Mr. Smock smiled. But he wasn't thinking only of the satisfaction of unveiling his beautiful portrait of George Grizzington, Bear Country's first president. He was also thinking of the delicious home-cooked dinner he would have that evening at the McBears' house. He lived alone, and he wasn't much of a cook. In fact, he had the same thing for dinner every night: a peanut-butter-and-honey sandwich. That wouldn't

have been so bad if he didn't also have a peanut-butter-and-honey sandwich every day for lunch. And breakfast, too. So, when the McBears had invited him to dinner, he'd accepted quicker than you can say "honey-baked salmon." Which, by the way, was exactly what Mrs. McBear was famous for cooking.

Mr. Honeycomb finally finished his speech and invited Mr. Smock to unveil his masterpiece. Mr. Smock rose and said to the audience, "It's a portrait of someone you will all recognize." Then he lifted the veil and draped it over the top of the easel.

Instantly a volley of flashes went off as the photographers took their pictures. The

only sounds at first were a few gasps of astonishment from the audience. Then some giggles. Giggles? Something was wrong...

Mr. Smock turned to look at his master-piece for the first time since its completion. His eyes widened in horror. It was gone! His beautiful portrait of George Grizzington had been replaced with a different one! And this one was *not* beautiful—not by any stretch of the imagination. In fact, it was

the most hideous portrait he had ever seen! The head was all lumpy and the eyes were bugging out. The nose was just a pair of nostrils, and the ears were missing. And who had ever heard of George Grizzington wearing a red sweatshirt?

Wait a minute! Mr. Smock looked more closely at that red sweatshirt and realized that the portrait was not of George Grizzington. But it was indeed of someone the audience recognized. For painted in large block letters across the sweatshirt was QUEENIE.

"I think it's kind of interesting," Babs

Bruno was saying to Ferdy Factual. "It must be modern art."

"I don't know how *modern* it is," sneered Ferdy. "But it certainly is *ugly*."

By now the giggling had turned into roaring laughter. Roaring laughter mixed with hoots, hollers, hisses, and boos. Reporters scribbled furiously on their notepads. Photographers and camerabears fell all over each other to get good shots of both stage and audience.

Mr. Smock waved his arms wildly at the audience. "This isn't my masterpiece!" he cried.

"No kidding!" yelled Too-Tall above the din. "It's your *mess*terpiece!" He settled back into his seat and surveyed the scene. "Ain't this beautiful?" he said to Smirk. "Look at Queenie's face. That crush of hers just crumbled into a million pieces!"

"Yeah," said Smirk. "I'll bet she'd like to rip that awful portrait into a million pieces, too!"

But just then Skuzz muttered, "Uh-oh. You got a problem, boss..."

"Are you kiddin', Skuzzo?" said Too-Tall. "Smooth sailing!"

"Look at the underside of the veil draped over the easel," said Skuzz. "It's white."

"Big deal," said Too-Tall. "So's my mama's aprons."

"That's exactly what I was just thinkin', boss," said Skuzz. "Smock's veil is blue. Remember how we covered your painting with your mom's apron before you smuggled it in here last night? It looks like you accidentally left the apron on when you switched your painting with his. You musta put Smock's veil right over the apron..."

Too-Tall took a closer look. His stomach went all queasy.

"I don't know, boss," Skuzz was saying. "Somebody's bound to notice sooner or later."

Vinnie leaned over to Too-Tall and whispered, "Don't give up hope, boss. Maybe everybody'll think your mom did it."

Someone did notice. Someone in the audience. And sooner rather than later.

Suddenly, Queenie dashed down the aisle. She leapt onto the stage and snatched the apron from the easel. "Aha!" she cried. She approached the audience, holding the apron high as flashes flashed and pens scribbled. She pointed a finger directly at Too-Tall.

"You did this!" she cried. "*You* stole Mr. Smock's masterpiece!"

Chapter 10
Dinner for Two

Queenie peered into the bathroom mirror as she adjusted her bead necklace. She wanted to look perfect for her big dinner date with Mr. Smock. He would be there any minute now.

She hoped he wouldn't be mad at her for tricking him into coming. Naturally, he had assumed that the invitation to dinner was from her parents and that she was only the messenger. She hadn't actually lied to him. When she'd invited him and he had replied, "Please tell your parents that I accept their

kind invitation," she had just run off without saying anything. She'd simply "forgotten" to mention that her parents would be out to dinner that night. Nor had she "remembered" to tell her parents that she'd invited Mr. Smock to dinner. And there was another convenient thing that had happened. Somehow it had just "worked out" that tonight was the night of the week when Bermuda always ate dinner early, then stayed glued to the TV set in Queenie's room for several hours watching her favorite shows, which included "Brainless" and "Sabrina the Teenage Bear." So it looked as though it would be just Mr. Smock and Queenie for dinner tonight!

Out on the porch, Mr. Smock pressed the doorbell and stepped back to wait. He was very relieved that this dinner was really going to happen. Earlier, as he had looked

at that hideous portrait of Queenie, it had occurred to him that the McBears might want to have him *for* dinner rather than *to* dinner. But now everything was fine: Too-Tall would probably get expelled, and he was sure Chief Bruno would find his masterpiece. (Even if Too-Tall had destroyed it, he could paint another one; the important thing was that nobody thought that he, Mr. Smock, had painted that horrible portrait of Queenie.)

Honey-baked salmon, thought Mr. Smock. He was more than ready for it. He was even

dressed up. Or, at least, neatly dressed. By his standards, that is. Ordinarily, his smock-jacket was covered with paint smears and crumbs from peanut-butter-and-honey sandwiches. Now it was covered only with paint smears, for he had carefully de-crumbed it. (The paint smears, of course, were permanent.)

Queenie answered the door. "I should have known you'd be fashionably late," she cooed. "You're *so* grown-up!"

"That's because I'm a grownup," said Mr. Smock.

Queenie blushed and giggled. "And you're *so* witty, too!" She grabbed his arm and pulled him into the living room.

"Where are your parents?" asked Mr. Smock, looking around.

"Oh, *them*...," said Queenie. "Well...er, uh...actually, they're out to dinner at the

Red Berry. So I guess it's just you and me."

Mr. Smock frowned. "But didn't you tell them I accepted the invitation?"

"No," said Queenie.

"Why not?"

"Because they never asked?" said Queenie, with a sheepish grin. "Anyway, I'm making honey-baked salmon. It should be ready soon."

Just then Mr. Smock smelled something burning. "Did you say the salmon would be ready soon?" he asked Queenie, who nodded. "Well, if you'd said that about twenty minutes ago, you'd have been right."

Now Queenie smelled it, too. "Oh, no!" she cried, and ran to the kitchen, with Mr. Smock right behind her.

Smoke was pouring out around the oven door. Spying a fire extinguisher on the wall, Mr. Smock grabbed it, flung open the oven

door, and doused the flames. He and Queenie stared down at the charred and oozing
mess in the pan.

Queenie smiled nervously. "How about
blackened honey-baked salmon?" she said.
"I could wash off the white stuff..."

But Mr. Smock wasn't listening. He was

too busy putting two and two together. Everything that had happened that week was falling into place. Queenie's dreamy stares, her Q & S artwork, her tricking him into dinner for two...And Too-Tall's behavior... He must be sweet on Queenie! Yes, that was it! Queenie had a crush on her art teacher, and Too-Tall had a crush on her!

"But you probably don't like blackened salmon," Queenie was saying. "Hey, I know! Let's go to the Burger Bear for dinner!" It had just occurred to her that that was a way for the other cubs to see her on her date with Mr. Smock. What an impression *that* would make!

"I think I'd better just go home," said Mr. Smock. "You know it was wrong to trick me like this, don't you, Queenie?"

The excited look was wiped right off Queenie's face. Tears welled up in her eyes.

"But...but I didn't lie...," she said.

"I'm very flattered that you wanted to have dinner with me, Queenie," said Mr. Smock gently. "But I think you'd better talk with your parents about the way you feel about me. I'm going to call them right now."

Mr. Smock bit his lip as the tears spilled from Queenie's eyes and ran down her face. She turned and trudged up the stairs toward her room.

Chapter 11
Easel Come, Easel Go

Mr. and Mrs. McBear weren't just angry at Queenie for tricking Mr. Smock. They were worried about her, too. She had never had a crush on a grownup before. Would she get over it as easily as she seemed to get over her other crushes?

When they got home, they found Queenie in her bedroom, talking excitedly with Bermuda. "Oh, hi, guys," she said, looking up. "We were just planning how I can get Too-Tall back. He must be pretty mad at me. I sure hope he doesn't get expelled for stealing Mr. Smock's masterpiece."

Mr. and Mrs. McBear glanced at each other and smiled. Apparently, Queenie's crushes on grownups were just like her crushes on cubs.

"Too-Tall isn't the only one who's mad at you," said Mr. McBear sternly.

"Er, uh...right," said Queenie. "I know I messed up by tricking Mr. Smock."

"You certainly did," said Mrs. McBear. "And also by not telling us you invited him. *And* by not getting permission to invite him in the first place. You can have a few more minutes with Bermuda. Then I want you downstairs to talk with us about your punishment."

"Okay, Mom," said Queenie.

Mrs. McBear went downstairs, but Mr. McBear hung back. "We're leaning toward grounding you for a week," he added.

Queenie shrugged. "Sounds fair, I guess."

Suddenly there was a shriek from downstairs, followed by Mrs. McBear's voice moaning, "Oh, my *good*ness!"

"Uh, better make that *two* weeks, Dad," said Queenie. "You haven't seen the kitchen yet."

Chapter 12
The Apology

Meanwhile, Mr. Smock was wondering what to do about Too-Tall. Earlier that day, he would have voted for expulsion. But now he was beginning to see it differently. For one thing, Too-Tall had already returned the

stolen painting. When Mr. Smock had gotten home from Queenie's, he'd found the painting on his doorstep. Draped over it for protection was another one of Too-Too's aprons. And taped to the frame was a handwritten note.

Dear Mr. Smock,

I'm sorry I stole your masterpiece. It was a pretty dumb thing to do. I guess love is blind, like they say.

Sincerely yours,
Too Tall Grizzly

P.S. My expulsion hearing is tomorrow after school. Maybe you could come and put in a good word for me?

P.P.S. Please return the apron to me. My mom's running kind of low on aprons.

Mr. Smock read the note again and chuckled. Clearly, the apology was just Too-Tall's way of trying to get out of being expelled. No, it wasn't the apology that impressed him. It was the condition of the painting that impressed him. Too-Tall had obviously gone out of his way to take good care of it. There wasn't a scratch or smudge on it. And the apron had been fastened to the frame with masking tape to keep it from slipping off.

Mr. Smock's mind wandered back to the day when Too-Tall had marched into art class and so proudly presented his still life. That painting, despite the purple oranges, showed a lot of talent and enthusiasm.

Too-Tall didn't take good care of my painting because he likes *me*, thought Mr. Smock. He did it because he likes *painting*.

And that was what convinced Mr. Smock to show up at Too-Tall's expulsion hearing.

Chapter 13
The Verdict

"Hey, boss," said Skuzz. "Look over there."

The gang was on the school playground for recess. Too-Tall looked to where Skuzz was pointing and saw Queenie prancing around in front of Cool Carl King. Bermuda, who stood next to Cool Carl, was glaring at her.

"Hey, she's flirtin' with Cool!" said Too-Tall.

"Ain't that rotten?" said Smirk.

"Yeah," said Vinnie. "And after everything she's done to you, boss."

"Get outta here!" said Too-Tall, with a laugh. "I think it's great!"

"Whaddya mean, great?" said Vinnie.

"She's not makin' me jealous now," replied Too-Tall, grinning. "She's *tryin'* to make me jealous. Like she used to. It's her way of makin' up with me."

"Congratulations, boss," said Skuzz. "Now if only Mr. Paint Smear would come through for ya..."

"Yeah," muttered Too-Tall, suddenly losing his smile. His expulsion hearing was only a few hours away. And there was no way to predict what would happen.

Later, when he went into Mr. Honeycomb's office with his parents, Too-Tall was relieved to see Mr. Smock sitting between the principal and Mr. Grizzmeyer. Mr. Honeycomb began by explaining that he himself favored expulsion, but that Mr. Grizzmeyer and Mr. Smock wanted only a one-week suspension.

Too-Tall suppressed a smile. He had expected Mr. Grizzmeyer to go easy on him, of course. Old Bullhorn coached all of Bear Country School's sports teams, and Too-Tall was his best player in every sport. It looked as if he'd gotten an extra break because the biggest football game of the year—the one against the Beartown Bullies—was just over a week away. But if Mr. Smock hadn't gone along with Mr. G, who knows what would have happened?

"So I insisted on a compromise," continued Mr. Honeycomb. "A *two*-week suspension."

Oh, no! thought Too-Tall. *Two weeks? I'll miss the big game!*

"However," said Mr. Honeycomb, "Mr. Smock suggested a much better compromise, one that truly fits the nature of your misbehavior in this case, Too-Tall. Instead of a second week's suspension, you must paint an oil painting of your own. That will give you at least a hint of how much work went into the painting you stole from Mr. Smock. And the result must meet with Mr. Smock's approval."

All right! thought Too-Tall. I've already *done* an oil painting of my own!

"Ah, but I just remembered something else that's bothering me," said Mr. Honeycomb. "The art supplies that were taken from the art closet without permission."

Too-Tall held his breath. Was this going to mess up the compromise?

"Don't worry about that, Mr. Honeycomb," said Mr. Smock. "I promised all my students supplies for oil paintings. I'll just figure that Too-Tall and his gang have used up half of the supplies they have coming to them. All right?"

"Well," said the principal, "if it's all right with you, Mr. Smock, I suppose it's all right with me, too."

Phew! thought Too-Tall. He looked over at Mr. Smock and managed to keep a straight face as the art teacher slipped him a wink.

Chapter 14
At Last! Honey-Baked Salmon!

The gang was waiting in the hall for Too-Tall. They let out a cheer the moment their boss told them about the suspension.

"Now we got a real shot at beatin' the Beartown Bullies!" said Skuzz.

"A shot?" protested Too-Tall. "The way I feel, I could beat 'em single-handed!"

Mr. Smock came walking by, and Two-Ton stopped him. "I just wanted to say thanks for goin' easy on my son," said Two-Ton. "He may be a knucklehead most of the time, but he's not really a bad cub. Son, don't you have something to say to Mr. Smock?"

"Sure, Pop," said Too-Tall. "Thanks for helpin' me out, Mr. Smock."

"Don't mention it," said the teacher.

"I really appreciate it—"

"Shush, boss!" hissed Vinnie. "He said not to mention it!"

"That's just an expression, birdbrain!" groaned Too-Tall.

"Well, I'm glad to be of help to a budding young artist," said Mr. Smock.

Two-Ton looked puzzled. "Budding young artist? Are you and me talkin' about the same cub?"

"Oh, yes, Mr. Grizzly," said Mr. Smock. "Too-Tall has natural talent as a painter." He turned back to Too-Tall. "Now, I realize you've already done an oil painting of your own. But if you'd be interested in doing another, I'll be glad to give you some pointers. I'll even supply the paints and equipment."

Too-Tall's eyes lit up. "You will?" He was about to blurt out, "Cool!" But he caught himself. In a casual tone of voice, he said, "That'd be okay, I guess."

"Good," said Mr. Smock. "We'll set up an appointment when your suspension is over."

"Oh, that reminds me," said Too-Too. "When Too-Tall's suspension is over, why don't you join us to watch the big football game against the Beartown Bullies? Afterward we can have dinner at our place. I'll make honey-baked salmon."

Now Mr. Smock's eyes lit up. "Why, I'd be delighted!" he said.

As the Grizzly family walked across the school parking lot to their car, Too-Tall was thinking about a lot of different things. About how lucky he was to get Queenie back as his on-again, off-again girlfriend. About how lucky he was to get only a week's suspension for the dumb stunt he'd pulled. And about how lucky he was to have a top-notch artist teach him about painting.

As he walked to his own car on the other side of the parking lot, Mr. Smock was also feeling lucky. But he wasn't thinking a lot of different things. He was thinking the same thing over and over again:

At last! Honey-baked salmon!

Stan and Jan Berenstain began writing and illustrating books for children in the early 1960s, when their two young sons were beginning to read. That marked the start of the best-selling Berenstain Bears series. Now, with more than one hundred books in print, videos, television shows, and even Berenstain Bears attractions at major amusement parks, it's hard to tell where the Bears end and the Berenstains begin!

Stan and Jan make their home in Bucks County, Pennsylvania, near their sons—Leo, a writer, and Michael, an illustrator—who are helping them with Big Chapter Books stories and pictures. They plan on writing and illustrating many more books for children, especially for their four grandchildren, who keep them well in touch with the kids of today.